The Little Ghost

Otfried Preussler

Translated by Anthea Bell
Illustrated by F. J. Tripp

ANDERSEN PRESS • LONDON

This edition first published in 2013 by
Andersen Press Limited
20 Vauxhall Bridge Road
London SW1V 2SA
www.andersenpress.co.uk

2 4 6 8 10 9 7 5 3 1

First published by Thienemann Verlag, 2001
Copyright © Thienemann Verlag, 2001

British Library Cataloguing in Publication Data available.

ISBN 978 1 849 397711

Printed and bound in Great Britain by CPI Group (UK) Ltd, Croydon, CR0 4YY

Otfried Preussler

The Little Ghost

Illustrated by F. J. Tripp

Contents

A Harmless Little Ghost

The little Ghost had lived in Eulenstein Castle for hundreds of years. He was one of those harmless little ghosts who haunt places by night, and never hurt anyone unless they are provoked.

During the day, he slept up in the attic in a heavy, iron-bound oak chest. The chest was well hidden behind one of the big chimneys. No one knew it really belonged to a ghost.

But at night, when the Town Hall clock struck twelve in the town of Eulenberg at the foot of the castle, the little Ghost woke up. On the very last stroke of twelve, he would open his eyes, stretch and yawn. Then he would put his hand under the old letters and legal documents he used for a pillow, and bring out a bunch of keys. There were thirteen keys; the little ghost always carried them around. He would wave them at the lid of the chest, and immediately the lid would begin to open of its own accord.

Now the little Ghost could climb out of the chest. He always bumped into the cobwebs; no human being had visited this remote attic for years, so it was covered with cobwebs and was dreadfully dusty. Even the cobwebs were full of dust. Showers of dust came tumbling down if anything touched them.

"*A-tishoo!*"

Every night, as the little Ghost climbed out of the chest, he would bump into the cobwebs, get some dust up his nose, and sneeze. He would shake himself once or twice, to make sure he was really awake. Then he would float out from behind the chimney and begin his nightly haunting.

Like all ghosts, he weighed nothing at all. He was light and airy as a wisp of mist. It was a good thing he never did his rounds without his bunch of thirteen keys, or the slightest breath of wind might have blown him away to goodness knows where.

However, that was not the only reason why the little Ghost always carried the bunch of keys. All he had to do was to wave them in the air, and every door and gate would open. Locked or bolted, latched or left ajar, they all opened of their own accord. The same thing happened with chests and cupboards, chests of drawers and trunks, even stove dampers, drawers, skylights, cellar windows and mousetraps. One wave of the bunch of keys, and they would open; a second wave, and they closed again.

The little Ghost was glad to have his bunch of keys. Life would be much harder without them, he used to think.

In bad weather, the little Ghost generally spent his waking hour haunting the rooms of the Castle Museum. They were full of old pictures and suits of armour, cannon and spears, swords and pistols. He would make the knights' helmets open and close with his bunch of keys; he would roll the cannonballs along the floor, making a lovely rumbling noise, and sometimes, if he felt like it, he talked to the ladies and gentlemen in the gilt-framed pictures in the Great Hall.

"Good evening, old fellow," he would say, coming to the portrait of Count George Casimir. George Casimir, who lived about five hundred and fifty years ago, was rather boorish in his ways. "Remember that night in October, when you bet your friends you'd catch me and throw me out of the window single-handed? I must say, that did annoy me. So you mustn't bear me a grudge for giving you such a scare. But did you have to jump out of the window, especially since the window was on the third floor? You were lucky to land softly in the mud in the moat. It might not have ended so well, though, you must admit..."

Or the little Ghost would bow to the portrait of the beautiful Countess Elizabeth Barbara. Some four hundred years ago, he had helped her find her precious gold earrings, when a magpie stole them from the window seat.

Or he would stop in front of the stout gentleman with the red whiskers and the lace collar on his leather waistcoat – the dreaded Swedish

General Torsten Torstenson, no less. Three hundred and twenty-five years ago General Torstenson and his army besieged Eulenstein Castle and the little town of Eulenberg. But he had been there only a few days when, one morning, he raised the siege and marched away with his soldiers.

"Well, General?" the little Ghost would say to Torstenson's portrait. "Do you know, some people are still trying to puzzle out what made you retreat in such a hurry. Just think what all those learned professors would say if they knew the truth! But don't you worry, General, I won't breathe a word. Well, I might tell my friend Toowhoo the owl one of these days; he likes stories. However, I don't suppose that will worry you now!"

The Torstenson Affair

Weather permitting, the little Ghost would go out of doors as soon as he left the attic. How good the cool night air smelled; he could breathe so easily out in the open, under the sky!

The little Ghost was particularly fond of moonlight nights. It was wonderful to dance on the silvery battlements, in the light of the moonbeams which made him shine whiter than a drift of snow.

The little Ghost would chuckle to himself, "*Wheeeee!* Eulenstein Castle is lovely in the moonlight. *Wheeeee!*"

Some nights the little Ghost would play with the bats, who came out of their holes at dusk and fluttered around the turrets of the castle. Sometimes he would watch the rats and mice scuttling in and out of the cellar windows, on other nights he would listen to the cats' concert, or catch a blundering moth in the hollow of his hand.

Best of all the little Ghost liked to visit his old friend, Toowhoo the owl. Toowhoo lived in a hollow oak right at the edge of the castle mound, where the rocks fell steeply down to the river. He was always glad to see the little Ghost. The owl was another who slept by day and only woke up at midnight. He was old and very wise, and liked people to speak respectfully to him. Even the little Ghost had to call him *Mr Toowhoo*, though they were great friends.

The little Ghost would sit on a branch beside Toowhoo the owl, and then they would tell stories to pass the time. Long stories and short ones, old stories and new ones, sad stories and

stories full of wonder –
any story that came into
their heads.

"I seem to remember
that you were going to
tell me a story about that
Swedish General," said
the owl one night when
the little Ghost was
visiting the hollow oak.
"Burstenson, wasn't that
his name?"

"Torstenson," said the
little Ghost. "Torsten
Torstenson."

"Go on then."

"Well, it was really very funny. It was three hundred and twenty-four years ago – no, wait a minute, it'll be three hundred and twenty-five years ago next month, on July 27th. This Torstenson came riding up one day with all his Swedish soldiers. Cavalry, infantry, artillery, thousands of officers and men. They camped all around the castle and the town. Then they dug trenches and built fortifications. And of course they brought up their wretched cannon and opened fire on the castle and the town of Eulenberg."

"That couldn't have been very pleasant," said Toowhoo the owl.

"Pleasant?" said the little Ghost. "It was awful, just awful! The cannon roaring and booming all day long and half the night. I'm no light sleeper, I'm glad to say, and it's not easy to disturb me. But I can tell you that it was more than I could bear. The thunder of those guns all the time, and the crashing, splintering noise when the cannonballs hit the walls. I put up with this appalling row for three days and nights, and then I'd had enough."

"But were you able to do anything about it?" asked Toowhoo the owl.

"Oh, yes! I spoke severely to this General Torstenson. The very next night I went to his tent and told him what I thought of him."

"Didn't he have any guards outside his tent?"

"Guards – yes, indeed! A lieutenant and twenty or twenty-five men. They drew their swords, held their pikes at the ready, and ordered me to stop. The lieutenant even drew his pistol and fired a shot at me. But as you know, swords and pikes cannot hurt me, and shots do me no harm; they just pass through me as if I were snow or mist: They couldn't stop me. So I flitted right into the General's tent."

"And once you were safe inside?" inquired the owl.

"Well, then I gave Torstenson a piece of my mind! 'If you value your life,' said I, waving my arms about and hissing horribly, 'if you value your life, raise this siege at once. Take your soldiers away, and never show your face here again!'"

"And what did the General do?"

"He stood there barefoot, in his lace-trimmed nightshirt. His teeth were chattering; he was scared stiff. Then he raised his hands in prayer,

begging for mercy. 'Spare me!' he cried. 'Spare me! I'll do anything you say!' So I grabbed him by the collar and gave him a good shaking. 'I should hope so!' I told him. 'First thing tomorrow you'll get out of here. And don't ever try coming back again! Don't ever think about it!'"

"Good gracious me! And what did Torstenson do next?"

"Torstenson did exactly what I told him. Next morning, the morning of July 27th, he and his army went away. They marched off as fast as they could go, cavalry, infantry, artillery – all of them, with General Torstenson in front, carrying his commander's baton."

"And he really never did come back again?" asked the owl.

"No, he never came back!" chuckled the little Ghost.

Don't Talk to me
About Daylight

The little Ghost had finished his tale of the great Swedish General Torsten Torstenson. The two friends perched on their branch in silence for a while, looking down into the valley, down at the river glimmering in the moonlight, the roofs and towers of the town of Eulenberg, with their weathercocks and chimney pots, their steep gables and bow windows. They could count the few lights still on and watch them go out, one by one – one here, another there.

The little Ghost at Eulenstein Castle heaved a sigh.

"Oh, how I wish I could see the town and the river by daylight," he said. "Not just at night when the moon is shining."

The owl hooted scornfully.

"Don't talk to me about daylight!" he said. "My eyes hurt just listening to you. In my opinion, moonlight is quite bright enough. I don't like anything brighter."

"And yet..." said the little Ghost, "and yet *I* would like to see the world in the daytime, at least once. Just so I'd know the difference! It must be so interesting...and so exciting..."

"Huh!" said the owl indignantly. "You're a sensible little Ghost – what can have put such a peculiar idea into your head? Believe me, my dear friend – I went out in the daytime once, and once was enough for me!"

The little Ghost pricked up his ears. "I never knew that! Tell me about it, Mr Toowhoo. Please tell me now!"

The owl ruffled up his feathers, twitched his ears, and shook himself once or twice. He did not seem too happy about telling this story.

"It was in my young days," he began. "At that time, I occasionally used to go on fairly long flights around Eulenstein Castle – partly on hunting expeditions, partly out of curiosity. Well, one night I forgot the time, and what do you think happened? Suddenly I realised that day was about to dawn. Just think! It was at least seven miles to Eulenstein. Would I get there before the sun rose? I flew as fast as my wings would carry me, but the sun was faster. It caught up with me when I was about halfway. I had to close my eyes; its bright rays blinded me. Do you know how it feels to fly blind?"

"I can imagine!" said the little Ghost.

"Dear me, no!" said Toowhoo the owl. "You can't imagine it if you haven't been through it yourself. Believe me, it was terrible. But the worst was yet to come!"

At this point, Toowhoo the owl saw fit to pause – in the first place to clear his throat, and in the second place to heighten the suspense. The little Ghost shifted impatiently up and down the oak branch.

"Well, what was the worst?" he asked.

"The crows – they were the worst!" said

Toowhoo the owl. "Suddenly I heard them cawing. There must have been a whole mob, thirty or forty of them. They caught sight of me and saw that I was  blind and helpless. They came flying up and swarmed around me, cawing the most awful things right into my ear. Such language! But that wasn't all! One of the crows actually dared to

peck me with his beak as he flew by. I couldn't defend myself; the others realised that, and then they all fell on me with beaks and claws. I thought it would be the end of me any minute. It was dreadful, my dear friend, really dreadful!

How I finally managed to get home, I have no idea. I got back to my tree more dead than alive. Once back here I was safe from the mob of crows, but you can imagine what a state I was in! I was in a bad way, my dear fellow, a very bad way!"

The owl flapped his wings, as if trying to shake off the memory of that very unhappy morning.

"And so," he finished, "I swore that in the future I would always take good care to be home before daybreak. We creatures of the night are not made for daylight. The same applies to you, my good friend; it applies to you in particular!"

Disappointments

But the little Ghost still wanted to see the world in daylight. During the next few days he thought about it more and more. *Never mind what Too-whoo the owl said. Nothing much could happen to me*, he thought. *And if anything should go wrong, I have my bunch of keys to help me. Anyway, nothing can harm me. So what could happen?*

Such thoughts generally lead to something. One night in late June, the little Ghost actually decided to make his wish come true. He knew exactly what he had to do.

"I must not lie down and go to sleep as usual at the end of my hour's haunting," he said to himself. "I must stay awake until daytime. That's all."

At the end of his hour's haunting the little Ghost always felt very tired. Sure enough, just before one o'clock that night, he felt an irresistible urge to yawn. At the same time he found his head and limbs were beginning to feel heavy.

He sat down on the edge of his oak chest – just to be on the safe side – and told himself, "Don't give up, little Ghost! Don't give up!"

But a little Ghost cannot go against his own nature. When the Town Hall clock struck one, and the hour's haunting was over, the little Ghost felt dizzy. He had to close his eyes for a moment, and when he opened them again everything was going around and around – the chimney, the moon outside the gabled window, the cobwebs, the rafters were all turning around and around and around until the little Ghost didn't know which was up and which was down. Then he lost his balance, toppled over backwards into his oak chest, and fell fast asleep.

He slept until midnight of the following night, and woke up disappointed and cross – cross with himself.

But he didn't want to give up hope so easily.

"Perhaps it will work out even better today," he said to himself.

"Anyway, I'll have another try."

But his second attempt failed too, just like the first. His third attempt to stay awake was no more successful either. *If only I knew how to manage it!* he thought on the fourth night.

The weather was bad that night. Rain beat on the roof, wind howled down the chimneys, water gurgled in the gutters. The little Ghost went off to the Castle Museum in a very bad temper. George Casimir and the other counts and knights looked mockingly at him – or so he thought – from their gilded frames. General Torstenson looked as though he would burst out laughing at any minute.

"Laughing at me, are you? That is all I need!" said the little Ghost crossly.

He was about to turn his back on General Torstenson, the knights and the noblemen, when he saw the gold watch lying in one of the glass cases. It was Torstenson's travelling alarm clock; in the haste of his departure he had lost it, and later, after many adventures, it had found its way to the Castle Museum, where it was kept as a souvenir. The little Ghost sometimes used to play with Torstenson's travelling alarm clock, so he knew how it worked. He began to make a new plan.

"You don't mind if I borrow your watch for a while, do you, Torstenson, old fellow?" he said with a grin. "I could use it, you know, I really could."

He waved his bunch of keys, opened the glass case and took out the watch. He wound it and hurried back to the attic with it. There, he climbed contentedly into his chest, setting the alarm for nine o'clock in the morning.

"If I put it under my ear," he said to himself, "I'm sure to wake up when the alarm goes off. It just can't fail!"

But again, the little Ghost seemed to have miscalculated. Sure enough, the General's alarm went off at nine o'clock in the morning, but the little Ghost never heard it. He simply went on sleeping till midnight. Not until the last stroke of twelve rang out from the Town Hall did he wake up.

I wish I knew why this happens! he thought. He tried using the alarm a second time, and then a third, but it never worked.

So the next night he decided to put Torstenson's gold watch back in the glass case – which was a good thing. For, in the meantime, the two museum curators had noticed that a valuable exhibit was missing, and there had been a tremendous upheaval. They had even informed the police.

"There must have been some cunning thieves at work here!" pronounced Chief Detective Sergeant Holzinger. "Forcing a case like this without leaving any trace behind. Only real experts can do that."

Now the gold watch was back in its case as if nothing had happened. The curators might scratch their heads and wonder about it the next morning, trying to puzzle out how it got there; the little Ghost didn't care, he had troubles of his own. He went to tell his friend Toowhoo the owl the whole story.

"Can you understand why the General's alarm failed to wake me up?" he asked.

Mr Toowhoo blinked, as if he had to think very hard before answering the little Ghost's question. But he was a wise old owl, so, of course, he knew that every ghost in the world has his own clock, and the ghost's awakening and falling asleep again depends entirely on the running of this clock.

"And your own particular clock, my friend," the owl *might* have said, "is, as you should know, the Town Hall clock down in Eulenberg. That clock, and that clock alone, decides the time you

wake up. Even if you could not hear the chimes you would have to obey them. You can't change that, no matter how much you want to, nor can the General's alarm clock. If you really desperately wanted to wake up at a different time, the only way to do it would be to put the Town Hall clock back or forward. But I would not advise it.

I think you would do much better to leave the whole idea well alone..."

Toowhoo the owl *might* have told the little Ghost all this, had he felt so inclined. But he thought it best to keep his knowledge to himself. The little Ghost just might manage to change the Town Hall clock, and who knew what would happen then?

No, it was really better not to tell the little Ghost anything about it.

"I tell you what, my dear friend," he said evasively. "In your position, I would resign myself to the fact that there are some things in the world which can't be changed. Night ghosts can't go haunting in the daytime, not ever. You had better accept that and be happy about it."

A Near Miracle

The little Ghost was very sad. He moped around for the next few nights. After his recent experiences, he began to think he would never be able to see the world by daylight. However, as everyone knows, wishes sometimes come true just when you least expect it.

It happened hardly a week after the little Ghost's conversation with Toowhoo the owl.

Once again the Town Hall clock struck twelve, and as usual, the little Ghost woke up on the last stroke. He rubbed his eyes and stretched, as he always did. Then he climbed out of his chest, bumped into the cobwebs, sneezed – "*A-tishoo!*" – and floated out from behind the chimney, rattling his bunch of keys.

But how different the attic looked today! It seemed much brighter than usual, and much larger.

There was golden moonlight streaming in through the chinks between the tiles on the roof. That must account for it.

Golden moonlight?

Moonlight is silver, sometimes with a tinge of blue. But golden...?

If it's not moonlight, thought the little Ghost, *then what is it?*

He flitted over to the nearest attic window, to look out – but then he shrank back, closing his eyes.

The strange light outside was so dazzlingly bright that the little Ghost had to get used to it gradually. Blinking cautiously, he peeped out of the window again. It took quite some time before he could open his eyes and take a good look.

"Oh!" he cried in amazement.

How bright the world was today! And how colourful! Up until then the little Ghost had always thought that trees were black and roofs were grey. Now he saw that they were really green and red.

Everything had its own particular colour!

Doors and window frames were painted brown; there were brightly patterned curtains in the houses. The gravel in the castle yard was yellow; the tufts of grass on the walls were a bright fresh green. A flag with red and gold stripes was flying from the top of the tower, and high above it all arched the glorious blue summer sky, bright and clear, with only a few little white clouds blowing over it like little fishing boats in a great sea.

"It's lovely, quite lovely!" cried the little Ghost in delight. He could not take his eyes off the scene. "Have I really woken up in daytime at last?"

He rubbed his eyes and pinched his nose. No, he was not dreaming!

"This is daylight! Broad daylight!" cried the little Ghost, quite beside himself with joy.

How and why his wish had come true, he had no idea.

Perhaps a miracle had happened.

Who could say…?

But it was all the same to the little Ghost.

At last I can see the world by daylight! he thought. *That's the main thing. There's no time to lose. I must have a closer look at Eulenstein Castle!*

Sun and Shade

The little Ghost hurried down the attic steps full of curiosity.

He floated down the main stairway, from the third floor to the second floor, from the second floor to the first floor, from the first floor to the ground floor. Then he flitted into the entrance hall which led to the castle yard.

But as chance would have it, that very morning Mr Thalmeyer, the head teacher, was taking a class of children around the Castle Museum. And it so happened that he and the schoolchildren came into the entrance hall from the opposite direction at that very moment.

When the children saw the little Ghost, the girls began to scream, and the boys shouted, "Mr Thalmeyer, there's a ghost! A ghost, Mr Thalmeyer!"

There was a fearful uproar in the entrance hall, and the little Ghost, who was not used to being shouted at by children, was so frightened

by the noise that he made his escape as fast as possible. He shot out of the door and into the castle yard.

The children thought the little Ghost was frightened of *them*.

"Come on!" cried some of the boys. "Run after it! Let's catch it!"

"Yes, catch it, catch it!" shouted the others. "Quick, before it gets away!"

Before Mr Thalmeyer could stop them, all thirty-seven children were chasing after the little Ghost. Whooping like Indians, they dashed through the hall and out of the door.

"Did you see it? Where did it go?" cried the children at the back.

"There it goes!" shouted the ones in front.

The little Ghost kept in the shadow of the castle walls as long as he could. Like all night creatures, he avoided bright sunlight, and anyway, he was thoroughly enjoying this game of hide-and-seek with the children.

Go on then, shout! he thought. *You needn't think I'm afraid of you!*

Once, he let the children come quite close. But as the nearest boys were about to grab him, he suddenly ducked, and his pursuers fell flat on their faces.

This is good fun! thought the little Ghost. *Let's do it again.*

The same trick worked a second time. But the third time, the little Ghost became careless. In dodging the children, he left the shadow of the walls and came out into the bright sunlight.

Then a strange thing happened.

As soon as the first sunbeam touched him, the little Ghost felt a violent blow on the head, which almost threw him to the ground. Crying out, he put his hands in front of his face and began reeling about.

"Look, look!" cried the children. "What happened to the ghost? It was white before, and now it has suddenly turned black! Black as a chimney sweep!"

The little Ghost heard the children shouting, but he did not understand what they were saying. He could feel that something he could not explain had happened to him. How was he to know that ghosts turn black at the first touch of a sunbeam?

I must get away! was his only clear thought. *I must get out of here.*

But where could he go in all this confusion?

Not back to the attic – the children were in the way.

The well in the middle of the yard! Suppose he went down the well?

He would be safe in the well. Safe from the children and the sunlight...

Quickly, the little Ghost made up his mind.

He hurried to the well and jumped in.

The children were very frightened when they saw him jump.

"Mr Thalmeyer!" they shouted. "Quick! Mr Thalmeyer! The ghost has jumped down the well!"

Mr Thalmeyer did not believe in ghosts. He thought that a real person must have fallen into the well.

"Oh dear, oh dear!" cried Mr Thalmeyer, wringing his hands. "Oh, what a catastrophe! We must call for help at once. Shout, children, shout!"

Mr Thalmeyer and the thirty-seven children shouted for help.

They shouted so loud that the castle caretaker and the two museum curators and all the people being shown around the castle came running up in alarm, asking what had happened.

"It's terrible!" stammered Mr Thalmeyer. "Someone has fallen into the well!"

"Not one of the children?" asked the castle caretaker, horrified.

"No, no, I'm happy to say. It was – it was..."

"Well, who was it?"

Mr Thalmeyer shrugged his shoulders.

"I don't really know who it was," he said. "But we all saw him fall – and we must do everything we can to get him out again."

Down the Well

The well was a good forty metres deep, and there was water at the bottom. The water was dark and cold. The little Ghost had no desire whatsoever to fall into this water. He found a ledge in the side of the well shaft, broad enough for him to sit on. He perched there, looking down at the dark mirror of the water below.

A black figure looked up at him. The black figure had white eyes, and a bunch of keys in its hand – a bunch of thirteen keys. Because of the keys, the little Ghost realised that the black figure in the water was his own reflection.

"Oh, look at me!" he cried, horrified. "I've turned black! Black all over! The only white bits of me are my eyes. See how they glare! They frighten me. I'm frightened of myself! Help!"

The little Ghost's head was still buzzing. He felt dreadfully miserable and tired.

"I wish I knew why I turned black," he said. And that dreadful blow on my head just now! I feel dizzy thinking about it. It must have been the sunlight that hit me. The sunlight probably turned me black too . . . If only I'd known this could happen, I'd have stayed quietly in my chest and I wouldn't have budged an inch . . . The little Ghost looked venomously at his own reflection. How awful if I have to spend the rest of my life as a black monster! Perhaps there's some way to put it right – a way to make me ghostly white again? I do hope so.

While the little Ghost crouched inside the well, worrying, the castle caretaker ran to his office and called the fire brigade.

Before long, a fire engine came dashing up to the castle gate, ringing its bells. Seven firemen and their captain sat inside.

The captain asked the castle caretaker and Mr Thalmeyer to tell him what happened.

"Obviously, gentlemen," he said, after a moment's reflection, putting two fingers to his golden captain's helmet, "one of my men must climb down the well and rescue the unfortunate victim."

He turned to the seven firemen.

"Well, who's going to volunteer?" he asked.

"I'll volunteer, sir!" said all seven firemen, touching their helmets.

The captain chose the smallest and thinnest of his men, because he seemed to be the best man for the job. The others hooked a long rope to his belt, and the captain fastened a lantern to it.

"Good luck!"

Slowly and carefully, the fireman climbed down the well on a rope ladder, while his comrades held the rope fastened to his belt.

The little Ghost saw the fireman, holding the lantern, climbing down the side of the well. He felt most uncomfortable. He knew exactly how soon the fireman would arrive and discover him.

And then what? thought the little Ghost.

He looked around the dark well shaft. Right opposite him he saw a low iron door in the side of the well. It was fastened with a heavy iron lock.

Where did this door lead?

Swiftly, the little Ghost waved his bunch of keys. The iron door opened, revealing a narrow underground passage.

A secret passage! thought the little Ghost.

He slipped in, and the iron door shut behind him as if nothing had happened.

Good! thought the little Ghost. *Excellent!*

Now they can search with their lanterns as long as they like. I'm safe here. And here I stay until midnight. Then I'll go back up the well again, and back to my attic, and that will be that.

The Secret Passage

The little Ghost had always believed that he could sleep properly only in the old oak chest. But as it turned out, that was not so; he could sleep perfectly well on the damp stone floor of the secret passage. So well that when he woke up, the little Ghost had some difficulty in remembering how he had got there.

This time he certainly could not have heard the clock strike twelve. No sound from the world above could be heard down here, but he was quite sure that it was twelve midnight. He felt really rested, just as he always did when he woke up at the last strike of twelve in his chest in the attic.

The only things he missed down here were the dust and the cobwebs.

"This is silly; there's nothing to tickle my nose!" he said. "I feel I've missed something if I don't sneeze when I wake up."

He had planned to get back into the castle up the well shaft, as he had decided yesterday. But just as he was going to open the iron door, he had a new idea. "Suppose I go along the passage to the other end? I'd like to see where it leads," he said.

The little Ghost was pleased with this new plan. He tucked the bunch of keys under his arm, and started off along the secret passage. He could see in the dark like a cat, so that was no problem. He floated further and further down the underground passage, until he came to a fork in the path.

The little Ghost stopped.

"Do I go left or right?" he wondered. "It's difficult to tell. I'd better count it off on the keys. Right – left – right – left – right – left –"

The keys settled for right. *Very well!* Without hesitating, the little Ghost floated down the right-hand passage. It was damp here. Damp and cold. Now and then, rats would whisk across his path. Or were they mice? They dashed out of the dark and immediately disappeared again. The little Ghost had no time to ask them where the passage led.

It must end somewhere! thought the little Ghost.

Soon he came to another fork in the path. He took the left-hand turn this time, to keep things simple. The passage began dividing more and more often. The little Ghost realised he was in the middle of a whole network of underground passages. Eulenstein Castle and its surroundings were riddled with them.

Think of the work, digging these passages! thought the little Ghost. *I don't envy the people who carved them out of the rock here. It must have been a really tough job.*

In many places the passage was caving in; here the little Ghost had to flit over mounds of rubble and debris. Once he came to a strong iron grating, fixed right across the passage, barring his way.

It was impossible to open it. But why bother? Ghosts can make themselves extremely thin if they wish. It was easy for the little Ghost to slip through the bars of the grating. A few yards further on, the passage seemed to be coming to an end. There was a narrow shaft upwards in the rock, with an iron trapdoor over the top.

I wonder where that leads? the little Ghost asked himself, and waved his bunch of thirteen keys.

The trapdoor opened upwards. Broad daylight shone in!

Goodness me! thought the little Ghost. *Isn't it the middle of the night?*

He put his head out through the trapdoor and looked around.

The first things he saw were two shiny black boots right in front of his nose. There was a man wearing the boots. He had a blue coat with shiny brass buttons. He also wore big white gloves and a white cap on his head.

The little Ghost had no idea that this man with the white cap was a traffic policeman – and the traffic policeman had no idea that the black creature who suddenly popped out of the ground, in the middle of the busiest crossing in town, was a little ghost. He thought it was a sewer cleaner.

"Are you out of your mind?" he asked, putting his hands on his hips. "What's the idea, eh? Lifting that lid, getting in the way of all the traffic! Get back down there at once, will you – and quick!"

The drivers waiting at the traffic junction could not understand why the policeman was keeping them waiting. Some of them grew impatient and began to hoot their horns. But the little Ghost did not like to be shouted at. It annoyed him. The policeman needed to be taught a lesson.

The little Ghost began to puff himself out until his head was as big and fat as a rain barrel. Then he pursed his lips and let the air out of his head again. It whooshed out like a balloon going down.

"*Whoo-ooo-ooo!*" The little Ghost blew the white cap off the policeman's head.

The poor policeman almost fainted with fright. He stood there staring; his face was as white as a sheet.

"That'll show you!" said the little Ghost with a chuckle.

Pleased, he went back into the underground passage. The trapdoor closed over him with a bang.

It took the traffic policeman some time to recover from his fright. It was at least five minutes before he managed to raise his arm and wave on the cars which were hooting at the crossing.

The Dark Unknown

For a whole week after the incident on the crossing, there was quite a stir in Eulenberg every day between twelve noon and one o'clock. At that time a black figure kept popping up out of the ground and frightening people all over the town.

On Tuesday it appeared among the stalls in the Market Place. The market women, who were not in general particularly squeamish, fled in all directions, screeching and yelling.

On Wednesday it visited the Golden Lion Inn,

and gave the landlord, his customers and his entire staff the fright of their lives.

On Thursday, the black figure with the terrifying white eyes was seen at the Municipal Gasworks.

On Friday, it caused indescribable confusion among a group of pupils at the girls' primary school, who were having a gym lesson in the playground.

Every day, in fact, the mysterious black figure was sure to turn up somewhere.

The *Eulenberg Advertiser* printed long and indignant articles, inquiring nastily how long the municipality intended to stand by without taking any action over these alarming activities.

The Mayor called a special meeting of the Town Council.

The Chief of Police and his officers discussed methods of catching the "Dark Unknown" night and day, but without any success.

No one in the whole town could offer any explanation of these daily incidents – not even Chief Detective Sergeant Holzinger, and he was famous for his cleverness in solving the most obscure problems in the least possible time.

Yet it was really quite simple.

The little Ghost was waking up at twelve noon instead of twelve midnight. He had lost himself so completely in the tangle of underground passages that he could not find his way back to the well in the castle yard. Every day, he had been trying one of the many passages and exits, hoping to get back to the castle.

Anyway, I don't mind seeing round the town a

bit, he thought. *It's a pity people always start running away as soon as they see me. I suppose it's because I look more like a monster than a ghost now. But I can't help it, can I?*

Sometimes the little Ghost felt homesick for his attic and his oak chest.

Sometimes he was sad to think that he might always have to haunt by day now, and never wake up at midnight again.

Eulenstein Castle was very beautiful in the light of the full moon, he thought with a sigh.

And then he would wonder for the hundredth time what on earth had happened to him.

"Can a night ghost turn into a daytime ghost, just like that?" he kept asking himself. "And if so, why did it happen to me? Things like that don't happen without any reason. There must be some reason – but I'm afraid I shall never find it out. And if someone could tell me, what good would it do? I must just put up with it, I suppose, and that's that."

In the Town Hall

On Sunday the little Ghost discovered a new way out of the underground passages. Like all the other ways out of this subterranean network, it was barred by a strong grating fixed firmly in the wall. But a few feet behind this particular grating there was another, and behind the second grating there was a third one. And behind the third grating there was a steel door with a safety lock.

What's all this? thought the little Ghost.

Dealing with the safety lock was easy. One wave of the bunch of keys, and the door was open. The little Ghost went through a coal cellar right into Eulenberg Town Hall. Then he floated up the cellar steps. His eyes were round with surprise when he suddenly found himself inside the Town Hall, with all its corridors and offices, its fine old stone stairway and the stained-glass windows shining in the midday sun.

On weekdays Eulenberg Town Hall was always full of life. Clerks and officials hurried from room to room, the Town Clerk bustled around with bundles of documents, all sorts of people waited to be admitted to the offices on all sorts of business. But today, at twelve noon on Sunday, there was no one around. The little Ghost could look over the Town Hall at his leisure. He opened all the doors and peeped into every room.

Making his way around the Town Hall, it struck him that all the rooms had the same picture stuck on the walls. It was bright and boldly drawn, and it represented – the Swedish General Torsten Torstenson! Big and pompous, he sat on a dapple-grey horse, with his commander's baton in his right hand. His green cloak billowed out behind him in the wind, and the feathers in his hat were as bright as his red whiskers.

Under the General's picture there was something printed in large letters. The little Ghost had never learned to read and write, so he did not know that all these pictures were really posters, upon which was printed:

— Sunday 27th July —
Historic Festival Performance on the occasion of

325th ANNIVERSARY

of the siege of Eulenberg by the Swedes

Genuine arms and costumes from the time of the 30-Year War.
476 participants, 28 horses, 2 cannons,
with music performed by the town band.

Starts at 11.30am in the Town Square.
We encourage as many visitors as possible.

"What is all this fuss about Torstenson?" said the little Ghost. "Sticking him up all over the place! One or two pictures – well, all right! But pictures of Torstenson in every room, along all the corridors, in every niche on the stairway! They really are overdoing it!"

In the City Treasurer's office, the little Ghost found a black ballpoint pen lying on a desk. He knew what he had to do in a flash.

Borrowing the pen, he added a big black beard to the picture of Torstenson in the Treasurer's office. Then he flitted into the next room, where he provided the General with an enormous bottle nose with a wart on it.

"It makes a change, anyway!" said the little Ghost, chuckling.

The little Ghost hurried from poster to poster as fast as he could go. With a few swift strokes here he gave Torstenson a pair of donkey's ears, there a patch over one eye like a pirate. He was having a wonderful time.

He thought of new, better scribbles: goats' horns, huge goggle eyes, a big paunch, antlers, a pipe puffing out clouds of tobacco smoke. Long shaggy hair, a ring through the nose, and even more ideas.

He was so absorbed that it was no wonder he forgot the time.

Suddenly, as the Town Hall clock was striking one, the little Ghost found himself in the Mayor's personal office.

It was high time for the little Ghost to find a place to sleep undisturbed for the next twenty-three hours.

I'll never get back to the secret passage, he thought, *it's much too far. I can feel myself turning dizzy already...*

In one corner of the panelled office stood an old iron-bound chest. Once it had been used to hold important letters and accounts. But now it was empty and it was only there for show.

That will do! thought the little Ghost.

With one last effort, he slipped into the chest. The lid closed over him, and he fell fast asleep.

Careful, Mr Mayor!

When the little Ghost woke up the next day, he heard the Mayor talking earnestly to someone in his office. Cautiously, he lifted the lid of the chest slightly and peered out.

There were three people in the Mayor's office. The Mayor himself, sitting at his desk in his big red leather armchair, and smoking a cigar. Opposite him, with his cap under his arm, stood the town's Chief of Police, and leaning by the window, arms folded over his chest, was Chief Detective Sergeant Holzinger.

It was obvious that the Mayor was in a very bad temper. "It's intolerable!" he said, bringing his fist down on the table. "I repeat, it's intolerable, to have someone scribbling over every poster in the Town Hall in the same low, mean way! I insist upon your finding this dauber. And pretty quick too! The good name of our home town is at stake. And if you can't bring it off, my good man" – here he turned to the Chief of Police – "then you're in the wrong job!"

The Chief of Police went very red. "Mr Mayor, you may rely upon the Eulenberg Town Police to do everything possible to apprehend the perpetrator of these outrages. I am sure it is only a matter of time. Hitherto, after all, we have solved all such cases with a few very minor, quite insignificant exceptions."

The Mayor puffed at his cigar. "I know all about your minor exceptions!" he grunted. "To think that this Dark Unknown is at large in the town, too. And all this with the three-hundred-and-twenty-fifth anniversary celebration only a week away! Don't you realise that the whole of Eulenberg will be a laughing stock if you can't stop this little game? Sometimes I wonder why we have a police force at all, I really do."

The Chief of Police bit his lip. What could he say to the Mayor? But the Mayor had already turned to Chief Detective Sergeant Holzinger.

"Well, Holzinger? Can't you suggest anything, instead of beating about the bush?"

Chief Detective Sergeant Holzinger took off his black horn-rimmed glasses and polished them.

"I fear this is far more difficult than any of us suspect," he said. "I shouldn't be surprised – no, I should not be at all surprised – to find that there was some connection between the Dark Unknown and all this."

He pointed to the ruined posters piled on the Mayor's desk.

The Mayor put down his cigar in surprise. "How did you work that out?"

"Well, it's hard to explain. I just have a sort of a feeling."

The Mayor scratched his ear. "And who is this Dark Unknown? Does your 'sort of a feeling' have anything to say on that point?"

Chief Detective Sergeant Holzinger held his glasses up to the light and examined them. He put them on again, shrugged his shoulders, and said, "My feeling tells me there's something uncanny about all these incidents."

"Oh no!" said the Mayor, much amused. "Next you'll be telling me there's a ghost around!"

"Well, and suppose there was?" asked Chief Detective Sergeant Holzinger.

The Mayor simply shook his head. "Ridiculous, Holzinger. Quite ridiculous! You may get children to swallow that sort of story, but not me. I don't believe in ghosts!"

Up to this point the little Ghost had been listening quietly to the conversation in the Mayor's office. But now he could restrain himself no longer. So the Mayor of Eulenberg didn't believe in ghosts? *Just wait, Mr Mayor!*

"*Whooooo!*" wailed the little Ghost in the empty chest.

The sound echoed around the room.

The Mayor, the Chief of Police and Chief Detective Sergeant Holzinger all jumped with fright.

"*Whoo-ooooo!*" wailed the little Ghost again.

Then he lifted the lid of the chest. Slowly, very slowly, moaning and groaning and rattling his bunch of keys, he began rising out of the chest.

His white eyes stared right into the face of his Lordship the Mayor.

"*Whoooo!*" he howled again, loudly and plaintively. "*Whooooo!*"

The Mayor broke out in a cold sweat. He dropped his cigar, gasping for breath. The Chief of Police's hair was standing on end, and so was Chief Detective Sergeant Holzinger's.

Unable to move, they stood watching as the little Ghost climbed from the chest and floated out of the room, rattling his keys.

Chaos and Confusion

Chief Detective Sergeant Holzinger was the first to recover his wits. Seconds after the little Ghost had left the Mayor's office, he threw open the door and dashed out into the corridor in pursuit. He saw the black figure with the bunch of keys disappearing round the corner.

"Stop!" he shouted. "Stay where you are! You are under arrest!"

However, the little Ghost did not have the least desire to be under arrest. He flitted away, chuckling to himself.

Mr Holzinger began shouting so loudly that it echoed through all the halls and passage ways.

"Look out! Everyone look out! The Dark Unknown is in the Town Hall. We mustn't let him escape! Stop him, stop him! Catch the Dark Unknown! Catch him, catch him!"

Most of the clerks and officials had gone home at midday. The few who were left in the Town Hall came running out of their rooms. Each was determined to catch the Dark Unknown.

"Did you hear that, Mr Muller? He's haunting the Town Hall now!"

"Hand me the scissors, will you, Miss Krause! It might be as well to be armed..."

"In my opinion, we ought to inform the police."

"An excellent idea, Mrs Schneider! Now, what was the number again? 2001 or 1002? Hello, hello, is that the police station? This is Lehmann speaking, Town Surveyor Lehmann. Kindly come to the Town Hall immediately, with all available men. The Dark Unknown...Did you get that? Yes, the Dark Unknown – he's turned up here. Come as quickly as you can."

Chief Detective Sergeant Holzinger led a search of the entire Town Hall for the Dark Unknown. Every room and every cupboard was investigated, every turn in the stairs, every nook and cranny. Even the bathrooms were not forgotten. But the Dark Unknown was nowhere to be found, not up in the attic nor down in the cellar. Even the police dog, Ajax, could find no trace of him.

"This is baffling!" said Mr Holzinger. "Such a thing has never happened to me before during my time with the force, and that's all of nineteen years."

But where was the little Ghost?

He had to go somewhere; even little ghosts can't dissolve into thin air.

However, there are other things they can do.

Originally, the little Ghost had intended to go back to the underground passage, but then the clerks and officials, egged on by Mr Holzinger, barred his way, and he escaped first up to the attic, and then into the clock tower. When the pursuers finally came up there (he could hear them clattering up the spiral staircase) he immediately slipped into the case of the Town Hall clock.

No one will think of looking for me inside the clock case, he thought to himself.

And indeed, no one *did* look for him there, not even Chief Detective Sergeant Holzinger. It was stuffy inside the Town Hall clock, and the constant whirring and clicking of the works disturbed the little Ghost, as he settled down to sleep.

"Life is a lot more pleasant for ghosts by night," he grumbled to himself. "I'd give anything to be a night ghost again. It's most uncomfortable here in the clock case. And very noisy!"

He put both hands over his ears, and soon fell into a deep sleep.

A Quiet Spot

At twelve noon the next day the little Ghost was rudely awakened. The bell of the Town Hall clock was striking right in his ear. Twelve blows on the head with a heavy hammer could hardly have hurt more.

Quick, down to the cellar! thought the little Ghost. And then I'll get out of the Town Hall the same way I got in, two days ago.

This was not as simple as the little Ghost imagined.

Whenever he thought the stairway was empty at last, and he could slip down to the cellar unnoticed, someone would come along just at the wrong moment, even if it was only the cleaning woman who swept the stairs and mopped the landings at lunchtime.

"I'll never get down there without a great deal of fuss, I can see that," said the little Ghost. "And I must say, I am getting tired of that sort of thing. All this excitement is not what I am used to. I'd better just wait here until next Sunday. Then there'll be no Mayors or cleaning women or clerks or policemen to bother me; they'll all be at home having their Sunday dinners, and I will have the whole Town Hall to myself. Yes, that's the sensible thing to do. And I won't climb into the clock case again, on account of that bell. I'll find a hiding place somewhere in the attic."

So the little Ghost spent the next few days and nights in the attic of Eulenberg Town Hall. He liked the place quite well. It had dust and cobwebs. It was true, the cobwebs hanging from the ceiling were not nearly as thick and long as the cobwebs in Eulenstein Castle, but still, the little Ghost almost felt at home.

The rest did him good, too. After his recent adventures he was thankful to be undisturbed.

There was no one to run away from him in fright, no one to chase him, no one wanting to catch him.

And the little Ghost was in no danger of getting bored.

As soon as he woke up, he would flit over to one of the attic windows and look out. He would gaze down on the Market Place where the women sat with their baskets full of vegetables, selling onions and carrots, radishes and celery, garlic and lettuce. Or he would look out the other side of the attic, and watch the fountain playing in the Town Hall Square, and a policeman in a white cap waving his arms a different way every few minutes. When he did that, cars would drive across the square, in both directions – trucks, vans, sports cars, sometimes a bus, a few cyclists too, and young men on motorbikes. Once there was a fire engine, and three or four times the yellow mail van.

"Everything is so odd down there!" said the little Ghost. "Is that man in the white cap a magician? He just waves his arms, and carriages come driving up. Strange carriages too, made of glass and metal, and without any horses. How can a carriage go without horses? Toowhoo the owl will never believe me when I tell him..."

Toowhoo the owl!

How long was it since the little Ghost last thought of him? Now he suddenly remembered his old friend again. "Goodness me, Toowhoo the owl! I'd almost forgotten him. Will I ever see him again? When I remember how Mr Toowhoo and I sat in the branches of the old oak tree, telling tales by moonlight, I feel very sad. I'm getting homesick again. Homesick for the good old days when I was a night ghost."

The Swedes on the March

The following Sunday there was great excitement in the town of Eulenberg. All the houses were decorated with greenery and flags. The municipal gardener had hung a huge pine wreath over the entrance of the Town Hall. It had a red plaque inside it bearing the numbers 325 in gold. Similar smaller plaques, each with a golden 325 on a red background, hung over most of the house doors and in the shop windows. It was easy to tell that Eulenberg was celebrating a three-hundred-and-twenty-fifth anniversary.

The first out-of-town visitors arrived quite early in the day. During the morning more and more people turned up. They came in crowds. Some of them came in cars, others by rail or bus. The Associated Youth Clubs

of Upper and Lower Geiselfing came clattering up in a farm wagon drawn by a tractor, gaily decorated with flowers and ribbons. Everyone wanted to see the great historical pageant. All the people hurried to the Town Hall Square.

The pageant began with the entry of the Swedish soldiers. They appeared from the Market Place. At the head marched three soldiers

bearing banners. The Harmony 1890 Male Voice Choir, armed with old pikes and muskets, followed them, dressed in infantry uniforms. The Swedish cavalry, nineteen men strong, were represented by the Eulenberg Riding Club. Appropriate military music was provided by the Town Band. They were dressed in wide breeches and brightly coloured waistcoats, hats with waving plumes, and they wore false beards. They played, alternately, the Finnish Cavalry March

and the General Torsten Torstenson Jubilee Fanfare (especially composed by the bandmaster for the celebration).

The Athletic Club and the Butcher Boys' Union, the Sales Clerks' Association and the Gardening Society, the Voluntary Fire Brigade, the *Nine Pins* Smoking and Bowling Club and the "Faithful and True" Old Soldiers' Fellowship, took the part of other troops in the Swedish army.

The General was even equipped with two cannon. Four strong horses were harnessed to each gun; they were really drayhorses, driven by their draymen. The draymen wore russet-brown tunics instead of their usual blue linen aprons. Anyone could see at a glance that they were Royal Swedish Artillerymen!

It was a good twenty minutes before the whole army had marched up to the Town Hall.

He should be coming any minute now – the famous commander, the dreaded General Torsten Torstenson!

The audience stood on tiptoe, craning their necks.

Here he came!

Big and heavy, he rode on his dapple-grey horse, his left hand on his hip, in his right hand his commander's baton. He waved it in acknowledgement of the applause.

How fine he looked with his green cloak, his red whiskers, and the gold lace on his plumed hat!

"Fabulous! Terrific!" shouted everyone, until the cheers echoed.

One out-of-town newspaper reporter asked who was playing the part of Torstenson.

"Don't you know *him*?" cried everyone. "Why, that's Mr Kumpfmuller, manager of the Joint Stock Brewery!"

"Are you surprised? Yes, Mr Kumpfmuller would have made a great general. Just see how real he looks. Even Torstenson himself can't have looked more like a Swedish General."

A fanfare of trumpets sounded.

Torstenson rode his horse into the middle of the square. He glanced up at the sky. The audience fell silent. The General cleared his throat and began to speak. His voice rang out over the Town Hall Square, loud and solemn:

"Here stand I in the King of Sweden's name.
I come to take this town, and yonder fort,
That dares defy us from its rocky mount..."

He went on for some time in this elevated vein, as befitted a famous commander. Then a young officer came rushing up (it was Mr Deuerlein, the pharmacist's assistant). He was supposed to have been sent by the General to demand the surrender of the town and the castle. But the commander of the Imperial forces had refused with a scornful laugh. If Torstenson wished to enter the town, he must make an appointment.

At his message, the General swelled with rage. He vowed that he was more determined than ever to raze the town and the castle to the ground. Then he made a signal with his baton in the direction of the two cannon, and uttered these terrible words: "My oath is sworn and may not be recalled! Now, cannon, open your mouths! Let shots ring forth!"

Here the Swedish gunners loaded their cannon and fired shot after shot; the guns boomed and roared. The audience yelled with delight. And no one noticed when the Town Hall clock started to strike twelve.

Single-Handed

Punctual as ever, the little Ghost woke up on the last stroke of twelve. He knew nothing of the great historical pageant going on outside the Town Hall. But he heard the thunder of Torstenson's guns – and looking out of the attic window in alarm, he saw the Town Hall Square swarming with soldiers.

"What's all this? What's going on?" he cried in amazement. "Have the Swedes come back again? What in the world are they doing here."

The little Ghost was very much annoyed. He

wished the Swedish army and their guns at the bottom of the sea. And suddenly, in the middle of the powder smoke, he saw a rider in a green cloak, sitting on a dapple-grey horse.

Good heavens – wasn't that Torstenson himself?

The General's hat, the lace collar, the fat face with the red whiskers... No doubt about it, it *was* Torstenson.

"This gets worse and worse!" said the little Ghost crossly. "Come back again, has he? He dares to show his face here! What is he thinking of? Does he imagine I'll put up with this sort of thing, just because he's a general? Well, he is very much mistaken!"

Now everything happened very fast.

The little Ghost flew headlong out of the attic window and down to the Town Hall Square, landing just where he intended – three feet away from Torstenson's dapple-grey horse.

"You, Torstenson!" he cried. "You must be crazy! Have you forgotten the solemn promise you made me, that night when you fell on your knees, wringing your hands and begging for mercy? Get out of here at once!"

Torstenson (or rather, Mr Kumpfmuller, Manager of the Joint Stock Brewery) was frightened out of his wits.

Utterly baffled, he stared down at the black figure with the white eyes. He could not imagine where it came from. And what did it want him to do?

"Well? Are you going of your own accord, or do I have to help you?"

Before Mr Kumpfmuller could reply, the little Ghost broke into a loud and fearsome howl. "*Wheeeee!*" he wailed. "*Whee-eeeee!*"

Mr Kumpfmuller's dapple-grey horse shied and reared. Then it turned and galloped away.

Mr Kumpfmuller dropped his baton and the reins. He almost slid down the horse's tail. It was only with great difficulty that he managed to stay in the saddle at all.

"*Whee-eee!*" howled the little Ghost, and again, "*Whee-eeeee!*"

No wonder the other horses became nervous. The Swedish cavalry mounts bolted, and so did the drayhorses, pulling the cannon after them. They chased after the General's horse at a mad gallop – right across the Town Hall Square, into the Market Place, and helter-skelter out of the town.

The Swedish infantry were also thrown into disarray. Soldiers and officers dropped their weapons, shrinking back in alarm from the furious black creature with the white eyes.

As for the audience...

Women began to scream, children howled. There was a great deal of shouting. "Move, will you? Get out of the way there!" The crush was terrible. People ran into houses and fled into side streets. They were all beside themselves with fright.

The little Ghost, however, had no intention of harming a hair on the spectators' heads. It was only the Swedes he was after.

"*Whee-eee*, you scoundrels! Go away, you and your spears and your swords and your guns. Go away! *Wheeeeeee!*"

The little Ghost routed them single-handed. Howling and hissing, he flew from one corner of the Town Hall Square to the other. Woe betide the poor Swedish soldier who did not move quickly enough! The little Ghost took him by the collar and shook him till his bones rattled. He did not rest until the entire Swedish army was well away, standard bearers, band and all.

"Victory!" he crowed. "Victory! Torstenson is beaten, the Swedes have run away. Eulenberg is saved once again. Victory!"

It was not quite the end of his hour's haunting yet. But for all his triumph, he felt tired and ready to drop. It is no small thing to put such a famous general and his army to right, single-handed.

I really think that will do for today! thought the little Ghost, deciding to go to bed, though it was not yet one o'clock.

As he happened to be near the pharmacist's house, and one of the cellar windows was open, he simply slipped in, and crept into the bottom drawer of an old chest of drawers. He was proud of his triumph, and quietly murmuring to himself, "Victory!", he fell asleep.

Hangover

The little Ghost woke up with a headache at twelve o'clock on Monday.

He felt weak and miserable.

All that exertion yesterday was bad for me, he thought. *But perhaps I just need a breath of fresh air. It's rather stuffy here.*

He climbed out of the chest of drawers and explored the basement of the pharmacy. He looked around the pantry, the coal cellar, the cellar where fruit was stored, and the woodpile. He ended up in the wine cellar.

"My goodness! All these bottles!" he wondered.

"It seems the people living in this house have a real thirst on them!"

The wine cellar had a narrow barred window looking out on the garden. The window was open. The little Ghost was just about to put his head through the bars and look outside, when he heard children's voices near the window. Hastily he drew his head back again.

The pharmacist's three children lay on the grass in the shade of the house, talking. The little Ghost could hear every word they said. Having nothing better to do, he listened.

One of the boys was called Herbert; he was eleven years old. The twins, Gunther and Jutta, were just nine.

Herbert, as usual, was doing most of the talking.

"You must admit it was fantastic!" said Herbert. "The Dark Unknown is really great! How they all ran! I nearly died laughing!"

Jutta was not so enthusiastic. "How can you think it was funny?! Aren't you sorry about the lovely pageant?"

"Hear, hear!" said Gunther. "If he hadn't butted in it would have been a wonderful show. Well, anyway, the beginning wasn't bad..."

"You know what I liked best?" asked Jutta. "I liked the way everything looked so real. Torstenson, for example. Didn't he look exactly like the picture in the Castle Museum? And anyone who didn't know that Mr Deuerlein is really Daddy's assistant might have taken him for a real Swedish officer."

"I wonder," said Gunther thoughtfully, "how much time and work it took, making four hundred and seventy-six Swedish uniforms. And where did they get the plumed hats and the weapons? It couldn't have been easy for the pageant producers to fit everyone out like that."

The little Ghost clung to the grating over the cellar window with both hands. He could hardly believe his ears.

If he understood the children in the garden correctly – and there was no doubt that he did understand them correctly – then it was not a real Swedish army he had routed yesterday at all. It was not the real Torstenson either!

Well, no, it *couldn't* have been the real Torstenson. It was all of three hundred and twenty-five years since General Torstenson besieged the town and Eulenstein Castle. No one lives to be as old as that, not even a General.

What have I done? thought the little Ghost, horrified. *Oh, dear! How could I be so stupid! And I thought I was such a hero ... A fine sort of hero! About the finest hero anyone could imagine!*

The little Ghost  was so cross he could have kicked himself. The more he thought about the whole affair, the worse he felt.

It's high time I went back home to Eulenstein Castle, he said to himself. Down here it's nothing but trouble, and I've had enough of it. I've had enough to last me the rest of my days! But before I get out of this town, I must tell these three children in the garden how it all happened. About the Swedes yesterday, and everything. Then they can tell everyone else. If it was my fault that the pageant was ruined, the people of Eulenberg ought to know how it appeared to me. After all, I have my good name to consider!

A Letter is Written

Swiftly and silently, the little Ghost slipped out into the garden and hid behind the nearest lilac bush. From there, in a friendly voice, he called out softly to the children. "Psst! Children! Don't be frightened! I have something to tell you – something very important. Please don't scream or run away. I won't hurt you."

Herbert, Gunther and Jutta looked around the garden, puzzled. They could not imagine who it was talking to them.

Jutta gave a little scream when she saw the black figure with white eyes slowly floating out from behind the lilacs, and beckoning to them. "Look – the Dark Unknown!"

"Yes, I'm afraid that's what they call me in Eulenberg," said the little Ghost. "I know all the people in the town are afraid of me. But I'm only an unhappy little Ghost, that's all, and I really am very sorry I ruined the pageant yesterday. I didn't mean any harm, it was just because I believed Torstenson and the Swedes were real..."

The pharmacist's children did not know what to do: scream and run away, or stay and listen.

"You're – you're a ghost?" asked Herbert doubtfully.

"Why are you black?" Gunther wanted to know. "I always thought ghosts were white."

"Only night ghosts are white," sighed the little Ghost.

"But what sort of a ghost are you?" asked Jutta.

"I've been a daytime ghost for the last two weeks, and the sunlight turned me black. But before that, when I was still a night ghost, I was as white as blossom, whiter than drifts of snow...I actually live up in Eulenstein Castle."

"But you've been down here haunting the town for quite a while," said Herbert.

"It was all an accident," said the little Ghost.

He looked pleadingly at the pharmacist's children. Then he told them his story, and explained about yesterday's misunderstanding. It was a painful subject, and he kept apologising.

"You don't know how sorry I am," he told them. "Or how much I'd like to tell the people of Eulenberg that I didn't mean any harm. But how can I do it?"

"You could write a letter to the Mayor," suggested Gunther.

"A letter – no, that's no good," said the little Ghost. He explained that he had never learned to read or write.

"Never mind!" said Jutta. "We can write!"

She ran indoors to fetch her fountain pen and some writing paper. Using the garden seat as a desk, she kneeled down and took the cap off the pen. "Right, you dictate."

So the little Ghost dictated, and Jutta wrote:

Dear Mr Mayor of Eulenberg,

I am very, very sorry about what happened to your great historical pageant yesterday.

Please let me explain…

It was quite a long letter. At the end, the little Ghost asked Jutta to read it back to him. Then she put some ink on his right thumb, and he solemnly signed the letter with his mark:

At once he realised he had forgotten something.

"Please could you add a little more at the end?" he asked Jutta. "Only a couple of sentences."

"Yes, of course," said Jutta.

She left one line free after the signature, in the correct manner, and the little Ghost dictated:

P.S.
I should be very grateful if you would have this letter printed in the Eulenberg Advertiser. And I give you my word that I will leave your town at noon tomorrow and will never come back again.

Don't Give Up

Jutta put the letter in an envelope and wrote the address.

"I suppose you're going back to Eulenstein Castle, if you're leaving the town tomorrow?" she asked.

"Yes, of course."

"And then you'll go back to being a ghost by night again, won't you?" said Gunther.

The little Ghost looked sadly at him. "I wish you were right... But I'm afraid there's no hope I'll ever be a night ghost again. That's all over and done with..."

The little Ghost began to cry. Big white tears dropped from his eyes and fell to the ground like hailstones – *drip, drop, drip, drop.*

The children watched him in horror.

"Whatever *is* the matter?" cried Herbert.

Gunther scratched his ear and said nothing.

Jutta was the only one who understood what was wrong. She tried to comfort the little Ghost. "Don't give up!" she said. "Let's try to think of some way we can help you; that would be more use."

The little Ghost shook his head. "No one can help me!" he sobbed. "If only I'd listened to Toowhoo the owl. He warned me!"

Suddenly he had an idea. Toowhoo the owl! Why hadn't he thought of him before?

"We ought to ask Toowhoo the owl!" he cried. "If anyone can solve my problem, he can...well, he doesn't know everything, but he knows a whole lot that other people don't. If you really want to help me, children, you must ask Toowhoo the owl!"

"Why don't you go and ask him yourself?" Gunther wanted to know.

"I can't. I'm a daytime ghost now, and he's

only awake at night. But he's my friend. He lives in the hollow oak at the far edge of the castle mound – it's easy to find it."

The children had often been for walks up to Eulenstein Castle with their parents, so it wasn't hard for the little Ghost to describe the way. And the children said it would not be very difficult for them to slip out of the house; they could manage that quite easily.

"But how do we get through the castle?" asked Herbert. "That's the only way to reach the oak tree. And everyone knows the castle gates are locked in the evening."

Gunther and Jutta looked dismayed. But the little Ghost had the answer.

"I'll lend you my bunch of thirteen keys," he said, and explained to the children about their magic powers. "You can easily get into the castle and out again, with my bunch of keys."

So the pharmacist's children promised the little Ghost to visit the hollow oak that night and to ask Toowhoo the owl for his advice.

"Oh, thank you!" said the little Ghost happily. He gave Herbert the bunch of keys. "Good luck – and don't forget: Toowhoo the owl is very particular. He likes people to be respectful, and you must always call him *Mr Toowhoo*. I just mention it so you'll know... Oh yes, and please don't send the letter to the Mayor today."

"No, no, if you say so," Herbert assured him. "But why not?"

"Because I promised the Mayor to leave Eulenberg the next day," said the little Ghost. "And now I may not be able to leave tomorrow."

Mr Toowhoo's Advice

That night, between eleven and half past eleven, the pharmacist's children tiptoed out of the house. Everything went smoothly; their parents never noticed a thing.

At this time of night the town of Eulenberg was fast asleep. Unobserved, the children hurried through side streets and narrow alleyways to the Upper Gate. Then they went along the footpath leading up to the castle. It was steep and stony; in the dark they stumbled over tree roots, stones and their own feet.

"Why not use my torch? Here it is!" said Gunther.

He was just going to switch it on, but Herbert stopped him. "No, don't. We mustn't give ourselves away."

"Oh, all right!" muttered Gunther. "I didn't mean any harm."

They stopped for a breather by the outer gate of the castle.

Jutta took a bag of barley sugar out of her pocket. "Have something to keep you going."

Jutta and the two boys felt their hearts beating fast. Gunther, of course, would have said it was only because of the climbing.

"Well, shall we try it?" asked Herbert after a while.

"Yes!" said Gunther and Jutta boldly.

The great moment had come. Herbert waved the bunch of thirteen keys. It worked. Silently and effortlessly, the heavy gates swung open.

"Come on, quickly!" said Herbert.

Once they were inside the castle yard, the gates closed behind them again.

"Brilliant!" said Gunther. "Nothing can go wrong now."

The middle and inner gates of the castle also obeyed the magic of the bunch of thirteen keys. Hesitantly at first, and then more boldly, the children walked forward. Once a bat flew close over their heads; once they startled a pair of rats in passing. The children were frightened, but they went on.

Around midnight they were standing in front of the hollow oak.

They hoped Toowhoo the owl would be at home! Gunther got out his torch and shone it into the branches. Up in the top of the tree they heard a hoarse voice, calling out something in owl language.

Gunther and Jutta could not understand, but Herbert did. "Switch off your torch. He says it's blinding him."

Gunther and Jutta were astonished. "Can you understand him?"

"Why, can't you?" asked Herbert. "Well then, it must have something to do with the keys."

Gunther and Jutta took hold of the bunch of keys, and found that they, too, could understand owl language.

"Who are you?" asked Toowhoo the owl. "And where did you come from?"

"We're the pharmacist's three children from the town of Eulenberg," said Herbert. "An old friend of yours sent us up here, Mr Toowhoo; he wants to be remembered to you."

"An old friend?" hooted the owl. "I didn't know I had any old friends in Eulenberg."

"It's the little Ghost!" said Gunther.

"You see, he's so unhappy," Jutta added, "and he needs your advice."

Now the owl pricked up his ears. "Why didn't you say so before? Wait a moment, I'll come down; then we can talk it over in peace."

Whoosh! He came sailing down and perched on the lowest branch of the oak tree.

"Now, tell me all about it, if you please."

Herbert, Gunther and Jutta told him the whole story. He listened in silence. Then he ruffled up his feathers and shook himself.

"Very sad, the whole thing is most unfortunate!" he hooted. "So that's why the little Ghost hasn't been to see me lately. Well, if you're asking me why he suddenly turned into a daytime ghost, I can only say, it must have had something to do with the clock!"

"What clock?" asked Gunther and Jutta at the same time.

"The Town Hall clock, of course." The owl gave them a brief explanation of the connection between the little Ghost and the Town Hall clock. "You should try to find out whether anyone stopped the Town Hall clock or put it back or forward two weeks ago," he added, very slowly and deliberately. "And if that did happen, then you should see to it that it is put right again. That's all I can say. Goodbye, lady and gentlemen; kindly remember me to the little Ghost and give him my best wishes."

With that he spread his wings, nodded to the pharmacist's children, and disappeared into the darkness.

Good News

No sooner had the Town Hall clock struck twelve the next day than the little Ghost rushed out through the cellar window into the pharmacist's garden, where Herbert and the twins were waiting for him.

"Well?" he cried excitedly. "Did it work out? Yes or no?"

"Don't worry, everything was fine!" said Herbert.

"I hope you'll be pleased," said Jutta, beaming. "It really does look as though we can help you."

"You can? Really?" The little Ghost was so happy to hear this good news that he began skipping for joy. "Go on, then, tell me," he begged them.

"Let's go into the summerhouse; no one will disturb us there," said Herbert. "But first I'll give you back your bunch of thirteen keys. Thank you very much for lending them to us."

"You're welcome; I hope they came in useful."

It was nice and quiet in the summerhouse. The four of them sat around the circular garden table like conspirators.

"Please go on! I want to know where I am!"

Herbert and the twins described their conversation with Toowhoo the owl, and told him that the owl suspected that the little Ghost's misfortune had some mysterious connection with the Town Hall clock.

"At first we couldn't make much out of this," Gunther admitted. "But then we decided that the best person to ask about the Town Hall clock would be Mr Zifferle, the master clock maker. So we went to see Mr Zifferle – and what do you think we discovered?"

"What?" asked the little Ghost.

"Mr Zifferle told us," said Jutta, "that sixteen days ago the Mayor asked him to overhaul the Town Hall clock. He stopped the clock at seven in the morning. Then he spent twelve hours working on it, until seven in the evening."

"And then, exactly twelve hours later," said Herbert in an important voice, "Mr Zifferle started the clock again – and he simply let it go on from where it had stopped in the morning. After all, the clock face shows the same time, whether it's seven in the morning or seven in the evening."

"But it's the same only on the face of the clock," Gunther put in. "And in fact the Town Hall clock has been twelve hours slow ever since. When it's twelve midnight, the clock strikes twelve noon, and when it's twelve noon, it strikes twelve midnight. No one in the town has noticed, because it hasn't made any difference to anyone – with one exception."

"And that's me!" cried the little Ghost, who had gradually pieced it all together. "It's because the Town Hall clock is twelve hours slow that I keep waking at midday instead of midnight!"

The children nodded.

They were sure this must be the explanation of the whole puzzle.

"Then you really think you can help me?"

"Yes, we do," said Herbert.

"We're going up the clock tower with Mr Zifferle at seven o'clock this evening," explained Gunther.

"And then," Jutta continued, "he will just put the hands of the clock forward twelve hours, so that it will tell the right time again."

"Is that all?" asked the little Ghost, amazed.

Yes, that was all, said the pharmacist's children. If that didn't work, they didn't know what else could be done.

"But it will work!"said Jutta confidently.

"Of course it will work," Gunther assured him.

"Oh, children!" sighed the little Ghost, rolling his white eyes. "I hope you're right. It would be so dreadful otherwise…"

Then he poured out his heart to the children, telling them how happy he would be to haunt the castle by night again, how he could think of nothing better than to be a night ghost. He talked and talked until his hour was nearly up.

Then he suddenly remembered his letter to the Mayor.

"You can send the letter this evening," he said. "Whether the Town Hall clock does the trick or not, I won't be in the town of Eulenberg this time tomorrow."

He was going to say goodbye and go back to the cellar. But Jutta would not let him. She insisted that the little Ghost mustn't sleep in the cellar this time; he could sleep in the summer-house instead. She made him a comfortable bed with her doll's pillows in a chest.

"Sleep well – and good luck when you wake up!" she said, before the lid closed over him on the stroke of one.

Goodbye, Little Ghost!

That evening, at seven o'clock, after sending the letter to the Mayor, the pharmacist's children climbed the Town Hall clock tower with Mr Zifferle, the master clock maker, and Mr Zifferle turned the hands of the clock twelve hours forward with a big spanner, until the time on the clock face showed the correct time of day.

"There we are!" he said when he had finished. "Let's hope that does the trick!"

The pharmacist's wife could not think why the children went to bed directly after supper that night. But Herbert and the twins had not had very much sleep the night before. They set the alarm clock for ten minutes to twelve, and then they were so tired that they fell fast asleep.

"I wish I knew what's come over those children," said the pharmacist's wife to her husband. She looked worried. "Are they going to be ill, or something? This is only the third time in their lives they've gone to bed without arguing. The first time they developed mumps the next day, and the second time they had scarlet fever. I do hope it's not going to be the measles or chickenpox this time."

Herbert and Gunther slept so soundly that the alarm did not wake them up.

But luckily Jutta woke up, and with some difficulty managed to rouse her brothers. "Come on, Gunther and Herbert, get up! It's nearly time. The clock will strike twelve any minute."

From their window the children could see the summerhouse. It was dark tonight; the moon was hidden behind thick clouds. But luckily there was a street light near the garden fence, which shone on the summerhouse.

"I hope we're not waiting for nothing," said Gunther doubtfully.

"So do I," said Herbert, just as doubtfully.

Only Jutta was convinced that everything would end well. She remained calm and confident – until the actual moment when the Town Hall clock started to strike. Then her heart began to thump wildly too. Breathlessly, she counted

the chimes. Four loud ones, twelve softer ones.
Midnight!

The children dared not move. They watched
the summerhouse.

Suddenly the door opened and a dark figure
flitted out. It was small and black, and it had

white eyes which gleamed in the dark like two
little silver moons.

"There he is!" cried Jutta, gulping with
delight. "There he is!"

The little Ghost floated up to their window. In
his left hand, he held the bunch of thirteen keys,
with his right he waved to the children. "Thank

you, children, thank you a thousand times for all your help! I can't tell you how happy you've made me. If I had a treasure to guard I would give it all to you. But as it is, I can only give you a good wish. So I wish that at least once in your lives, you may be as happy as I am now."

"Thank you, dear," said Jutta, and none of the children thought it odd for her to call him dear.

The little Ghost did not seem to mind either.

"You don't mind if I say goodbye now, do you?" he said. "I do want to get back to Eulenstein Castle. I can hardly wait to be home again."

"No, of course we don't mind," said Gunther.

"Don't let us keep you," added Herbert, "we know how you feel."

Moonlight Again

The little Ghost floated home, over the roofs of the sleeping town, to the Town Hall, from the Town Hall over the Market Place to the Upper Gate, from the Upper Gate to the castle.

"Goodbye down there, good people of Eulenberg!" he said. "I've made a lot of trouble for you these last two weeks, but you're rid of me now, and that's the main thing. At any rate, I'll never show myself in the town again. From now on I will stay where I belong. Nothing will ever lure me away from my castle again, not even my own curiosity!"

The little Ghost circled the castle walls, the tower and the Great Hall three times. Everything was exactly the same, though it seemed to him *ages since he had been there last.*

Shall I go and pay my respects to the General? he thought. No, that can wait until the next rainy night. I have something much more important to do tonight.

Toowhoo the owl sat in the hollow oak; he was not in the least surprised to see the little Ghost float up and alight on the branch beside him.

"Do you mind if I sit here, Mr Toowhoo?"

"With the greatest of pleasure!"

The two friends perched side by side for a while in silence.

"They managed to help you, didn't they?" asked the owl at last.

"Yes, as you see," replied the little Ghost. "The advice you gave Jutta and her brothers yesterday was excellent. Thank you very much."

"Not at all, not at all, my dear fellow." The owl ruffled up his feathers. "To tell you the truth, it was pure self-interest..."

"Self-interest?"

"Pure self-interest!" repeated the owl, nodding his head emphatically. "I was beginning to get bored without you. Life is a great deal more interesting when one has someone to talk to. You must have had a lot of adventures down in Eulenberg. Please tell me about them!"

"As you wish!" said the little Ghost.

He was just about to embark on a description of his adventures in the town – how he frightened the policeman and the market women, how he got inside the Town Hall, and about Torstenson and the Swedish soldiers who were not Swedish soldiers after all.

But then something unexpected happened, something that stopped him before he started to tell his story. Suddenly, the moon came out from behind the thick black clouds that covered the sky. It was a big, round moon, a disk of shining silver.

A silver moonbeam fell on the little Ghost.

And the little Ghost felt wonderfully well, light and airy, lighter and airier than ever before.

Then he suddenly noticed: he was not a black ghost any more! He was shining again. He was a white night ghost again!

"I'm ghostly white!" he cried in sheer delight. "I'm a night ghost, a ghostly white night ghost!"

Toowhoo the owl laughed.

"Are you surprised?" he said. "It's all perfectly natural, my friend. It was the sun that turned you black, and now the moon has turned you white again. That's all there is to it. Don't you think it's time you calmed down again?"

But the little Ghost was quite beside himself with joy. He did not listen to Toowhoo the owl. He couldn't calm down.

He danced on the castle walls till the end of his haunting hour. He floated around the battlements in the light of the moon.

He was so glad to be ghostly white again, just like he used to be.

White as blossom.

Whiter than a drift of snow.

The Dragonsitter

Josh Lacey
Illustrated by Garry Parsons

A hilarious novel for younger readers by the author of the Grk books.

'Dear Uncle Morton. You'd better get on a plane right now and come back here. Your dragon has eaten Jemima. Emily loved that rabbit.'

It had sounded so easy: Edward was going to look after Uncle Morton's unusual pet for a week while he went on holiday. But soon the fridge is empty, the curtains are blazing, and the postman is fleeing down the garden path.

'A witty book that deserves to be read and reread.'
Books for Keeps

9781849394192 £4.99

By MICHAEL ROSEN
Illustrated by TONY ROSS

On an ordinary morning, in an ordinary flat, an up-till-now perfectly ordinary Bertha does an extraordinary burp. A burp so extraordinary, it knocks things over. A burp so humongously big that very soon it's causing havoc in the school canteen, the playground, not to mention her grandad's apple trees . . . Such a burptastic secret cannot stay quiet for long. And soon enough it lands Bertha her very own celebrity stardom . . . but is it all just a lot of hot air?

'Harks back, like Horrid Henry, to the comic strips of Dennis the Menace or Minnie the Minx' *Telegraph*

9781849394062 £4.99

AUNT
SEVERE
and the
DRAGONS

by Nick Garlick
Illustrations by Nick Maland

When Daniel's explorer parents vanish, he has to live with his strict and rather strange Aunt Severe.

But just when everything seems to be going wrong for Daniel, he meets four dragons hiding in the garden. They tell him about their lost magic book, The Spelldocious. But as soon as they leave the garden three of the dragons are captured by evil Gotcha Grabber, who throws them into his zoo.

With the help of Dud, a rather clumsy dragon, Daniel must try to rescue them and find the missing Spelldocious.

Nick Maland won the Booktrust Early Years Award and was shortlisted for Mother Goose Best Newcomer.

9781849390552 £4.99

DAMIAN DROOTH
SUPERSLEUTH
ACE DETECTIVE

by Barbara Mitchelhill

with illustrations by
Tony Ross

Damian Drooth is a super sleuth, a number
one detective, a kid with a nose for trouble.
And here in this fantastic bumper edition are
three of his hilarious stories:

*The Case of the
Disappearing Daughter,
How to Be a Detective*
and *The Case of the
Popstar's Wedding.*

'Madcap cartoon-
sketch humour'
TES

9781849390972 £5.99

Pillywiggins
and the
Tree Witch
JULIA JARMAN

A magical story of towering tree witches and tricksy fairies.

When Natasha moves to a new house, she discovers a statue of a fairy in her garden beneath a huge menacing fir tree, which Natasha is sure is a witch. Gradually, with the help of a local boy, she unravels an ancient story that fairies stole the witch's baby and as revenge she turned a fairy to stone. Natasha realises that the only way to free the stone fairy, Pillywiggins, is to go into Fairy Land herself and rescue the witch's baby. But legend says that any human who enters Fairy Land may age decades or never come out at all.

9781849390187 £4.99